For Matt, who called
her by name

Balzer + Bray is an imprint of HarperCollins Publishers.

Swatch: The Girl Who Loved Color
Copyright © 2016 by Julia Denos
All rights reserved. Manufactured in China.

ISBN 978-0-06-236638-2

The artist used watercolor, pen and ink and pencil with Adobe Photoshop to create the illustrations for this book.
Typography by Martha Rago
15 16 17 18 19   SCP   10 9 8 7 6 5 4 3 2 1
❖
First Edition

SWATCH

The Girl Who Loved Color

JULIA DENOS

Balzer + Bray
An Imprint of HarperCollinsPublishers

IN A PLACE where colors ran wild,
there lived a girl who was wilder still.

Her name was Swatch, and
she was a color tamer.

She was small, but she was not afraid.

She could run with
the wildest shades.
Train them to dance

and do magic.

With a little patience,
she learned to hunt the rare ones.

Bravest Green shot up
the first week of March.

In-Between Gray lived
on her kitten's leg.

Rumble-Tumble Pink rolled through the sky on the heels of outgoing thunderstorms.

When she called them by name, they would come to her, because Swatch loved color and color loved Swatch back.

Swatch had never thought of capturing a color until
the day she lured **Just-Laid Blue** straight from its
nest and into a jam jar.

"Stay," Swatch said,
and the color stayed.

How beautiful it looked behind glass!
"You could use a friend," she said to Blue.

So she caught one more. Then another.

And another.

Soon Swatch's room was full to bursting. The colors circled, restless in their jars. They were magnificent . . . but there was still one color left to catch.

Morning came, and there it was, fast fading and fierce,
the King of All Yellows, blooming in the sidewalk crack
in spite of the shadows. Swatch was ready. . . . At last,
Yellowest Yellow would be hers.

Suddenly she heard a small sound.

"Ahem," said Yellowest Yellow. "What are you doing?"

Swatch had never *asked* if a color wanted taming.

"Yellowest Yellow," she asked politely, "would you like to climb into this jar? You could sit on a shelf, right next to Blue. You could make Green together all day long if you wanted! I'll poke holes in the top, and I'll feed you dinner."

But Yellow, knowing that was no way to live, said, "No thank you."
And Swatch, who could have scooped it up anyway,
said, "OK."

Given that small
but kindly allowance . . .

It GREW and YAWNED
and STRETCHED and TWIRLED.

It **BLOOMED** and *WHIRLED*
and LEAKED and *SWIRLED*,
SPREADING, **BILLOWING**, *TWISTING*,
up, up, **UP!**

It sprouted ears!
And pointy teeth!
It was as big as a house!

"ROOOOOO

AAAAAARRRRRR, "

went Yellowest Yellow.

Swatch felt small.

Her jar seemed silly.

She had forgotten colors were wild,

so she shut her eyes and prepared to be eaten.

Then Swatch heard something
sweet and warbling,
like a fleet of canaries.
She smelled something
warm and buttery,
like breakfast!
Then something
swished against her knee,
purring and soft
and just like home.

So she opened her eyes. . . .

She reached out her hand. . . .

And stretching from her tiptoes she found
she could indeed touch Yellow.

"Hold on," Yellow said,
and it pulled her **up** . . .

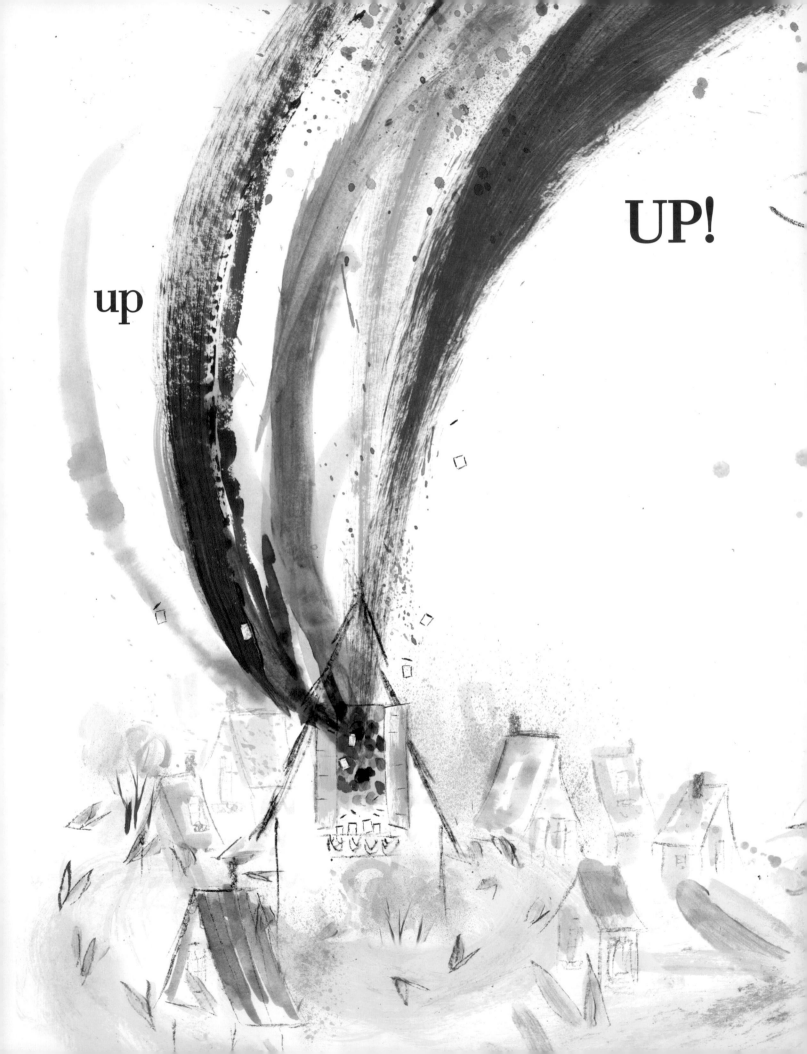

up

UP!

High up over the rooftops,
she called her colors by name
and they came to her.

Together they made a masterpiece.